P9-BZK-463

FIONA
THE HIPPO

NEW YORK TIMES BESTSELLING ILLUSTRATOR

RICHARD COWDREY

This book is dedicated to Henry.

ZONDERKIDZ

Fiona the Hippo

This title is also available as a Zondervan ebook.

Requests for information should be addressed to:

Zonderkidz, 3900 *Sparks Dr. SE, Grand Rapids, Michigan 49546*

ISBN 978-0-310-76639-1

Illustrated by: Richard Cowdrey
Contributors: Barbara Herndon and Mary Hassinger
Design: Cindy Davis

Printed in China

18 19 20 21 22 23 /DSC/ 22 21 20 19 18 17 16 15 14 13 12 11 10 9 8 7 6 5 4 3 2 1

On a cold winter's night, a baby hippo was born.

"Have you heard?"
"She's here?"
"Already?"

"Yes!!!"
"I haven't seen her!"
"Have you seen her?"

TEAM
FIONA
TEAM
FIONA
TEAM
FIONA

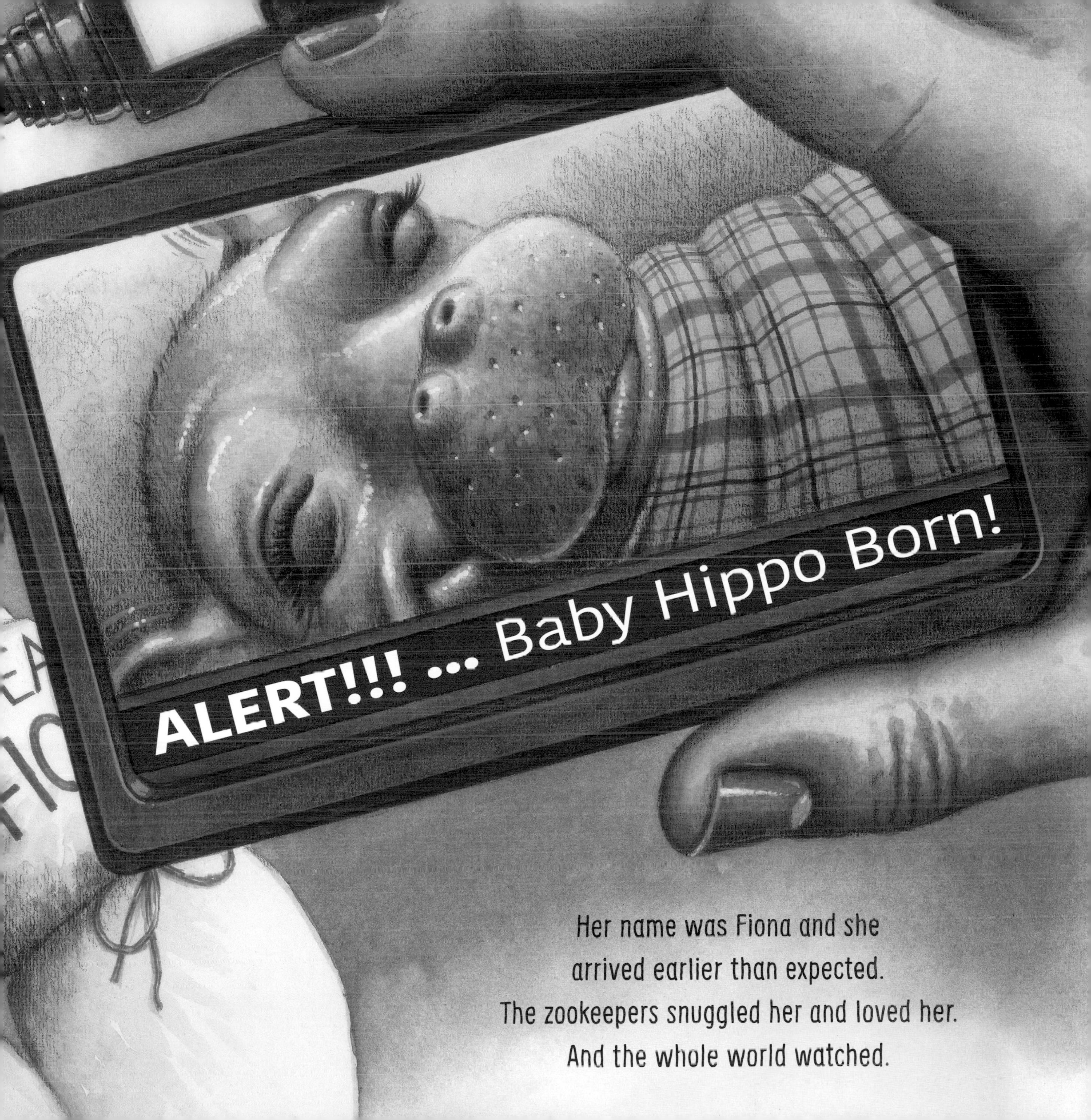

Her name was Fiona and she
arrived earlier than expected.
The zookeepers snuggled her and loved her.
And the whole world watched.

"There she is!"
"Really cute!"
"And kind of slimy!" said Ostrich,
as she and her friends peeked
at the littlest hippo in the world.

Fiona had to learn to eat from a bottle, just like other babies in the zoo. And when she was ready, she let out a snort, wiggled her ears, and said, "I've got this!"

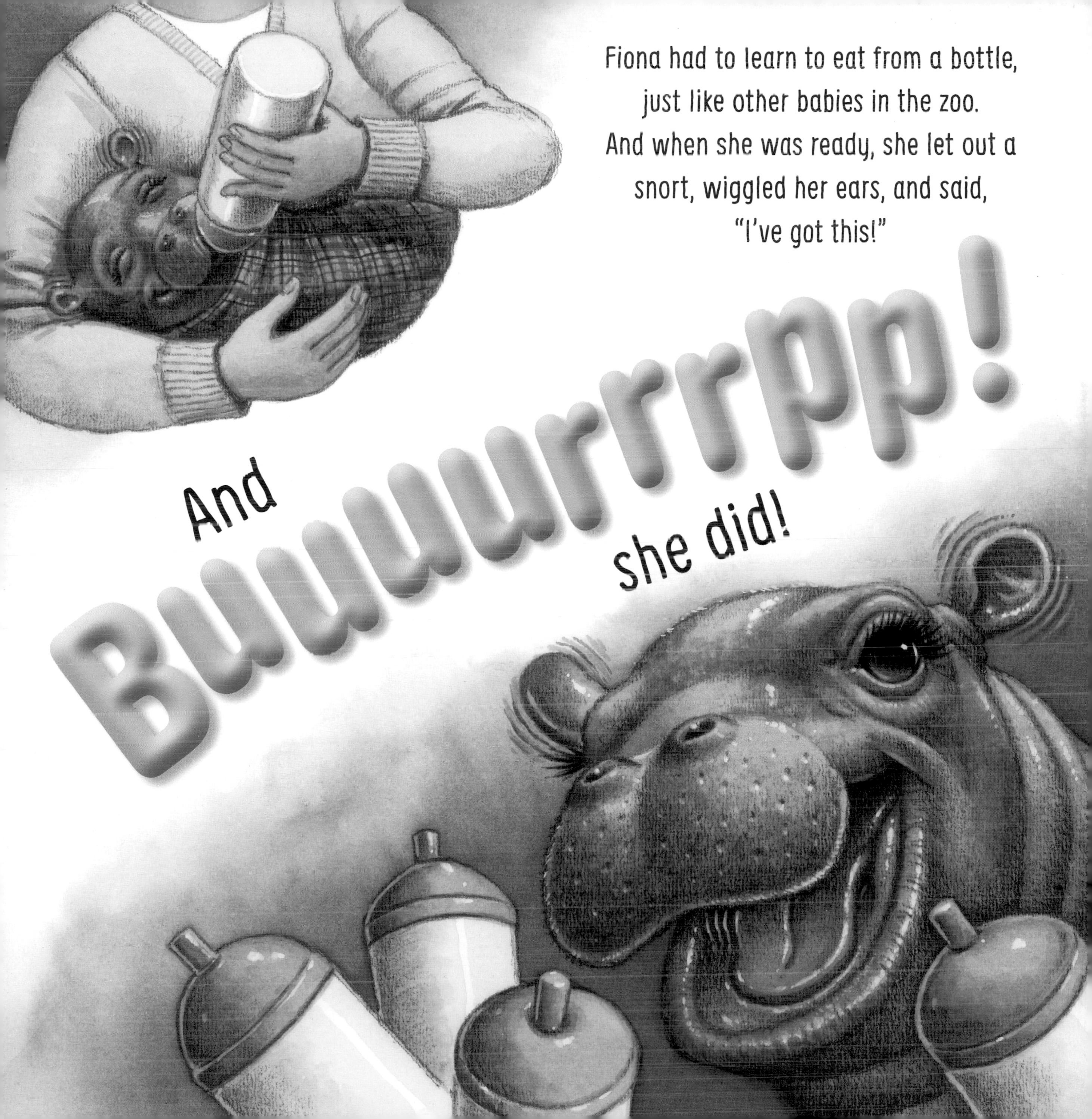

Fiona grew stronger and it was time
to learn to walk, just like other babies in the zoo.

And when she was ready, she let out a snort,
wiggled her ears, and said, "I've got this!"

And

**WOBBLE-
WOBBLE
PLOP!**

She tried over and over,
until she did.

Little Fiona grew bigger still,
and it was time to learn to swim,
just like other babies in the zoo.

And when she was ready, she
let out a snort, wiggled her
ears, and said, "I've got this!"

And STEP
by
STEP...

SPLASH!
She did!

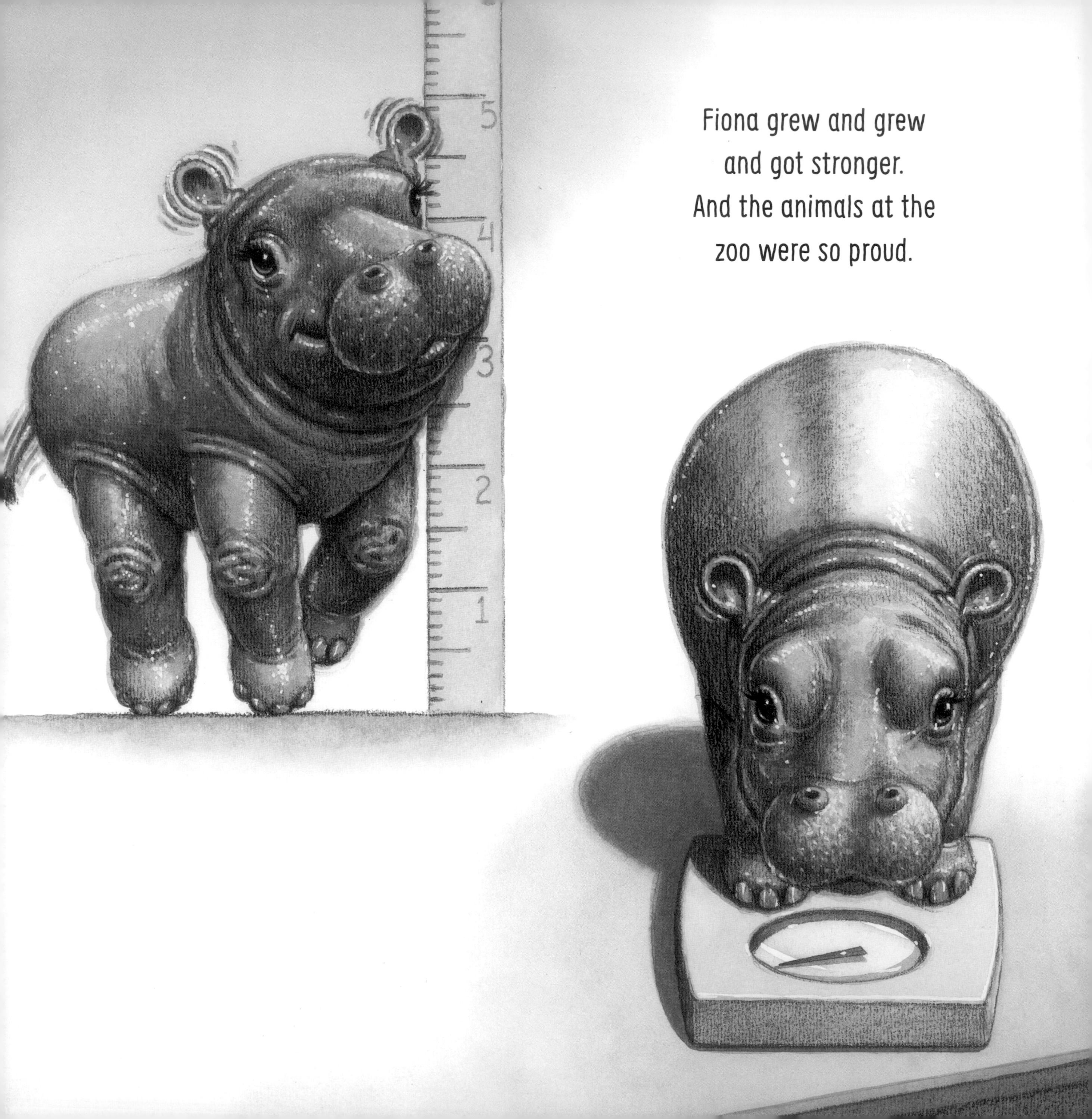

Fiona grew and grew
and got stronger.
And the animals at the
zoo were so proud.

"Look at our baby."

"So roly-poly!"

"When can she come out to play?"

But Fiona was busy.
She was growing and learning
about new things every day ...

I Like BUBBLES!

As the animals in
the zoo watched,
and the zookeepers watched,
the whole world watched Fiona too.

Soon the little hippo had a
mountain of fan mail that said,
"Congratulations, Fiona!"
"You are amazing!"
"We love you, little baby hippo!"

F
Fiona
FIONA
LOVE
U
AMAZING!!!
NGRATULATIONS!!

Then one day, after she was done eating and walking and swimming, Fiona said, "I want to be in the water with THEM!" She looked at the two big hippos swimming in the pool. "I want my mama and daddy."

Fiona was finally strong enough to swim with her parents.
And she was ready! She let out a snort, wiggled her ears, and said,
"I've got this!" and she swam with her mama for the first time.
"Wow, will my teeth get that big?" she asked excitedly.

Fiona went swimming
with her daddy too.
"Wow, will my bottom get that big?"
She giggled playfully.

Fiona loved her family,
and life was good for the little hippo.

But something was missing. As much as Fiona loved her mama and daddy, she wanted something more. “I wish I had some friends to play with,” she said.

"Did you hear that?"

"It's our turn to play with the baby!"

"It's about time!"

And one-by-one the animals joined their new friend Fiona for the biggest pool party the zoo had ever seen!

That night, Fiona snuggled up with her family.
She was bigger. She was stronger. She was happy. And Fiona was loved.
"Go to sleep, little hippo," said her mama.
"Your next big adventure is right around the corner."
As Fiona drifted off to sleep, she whispered,
"I've got this." And she did.

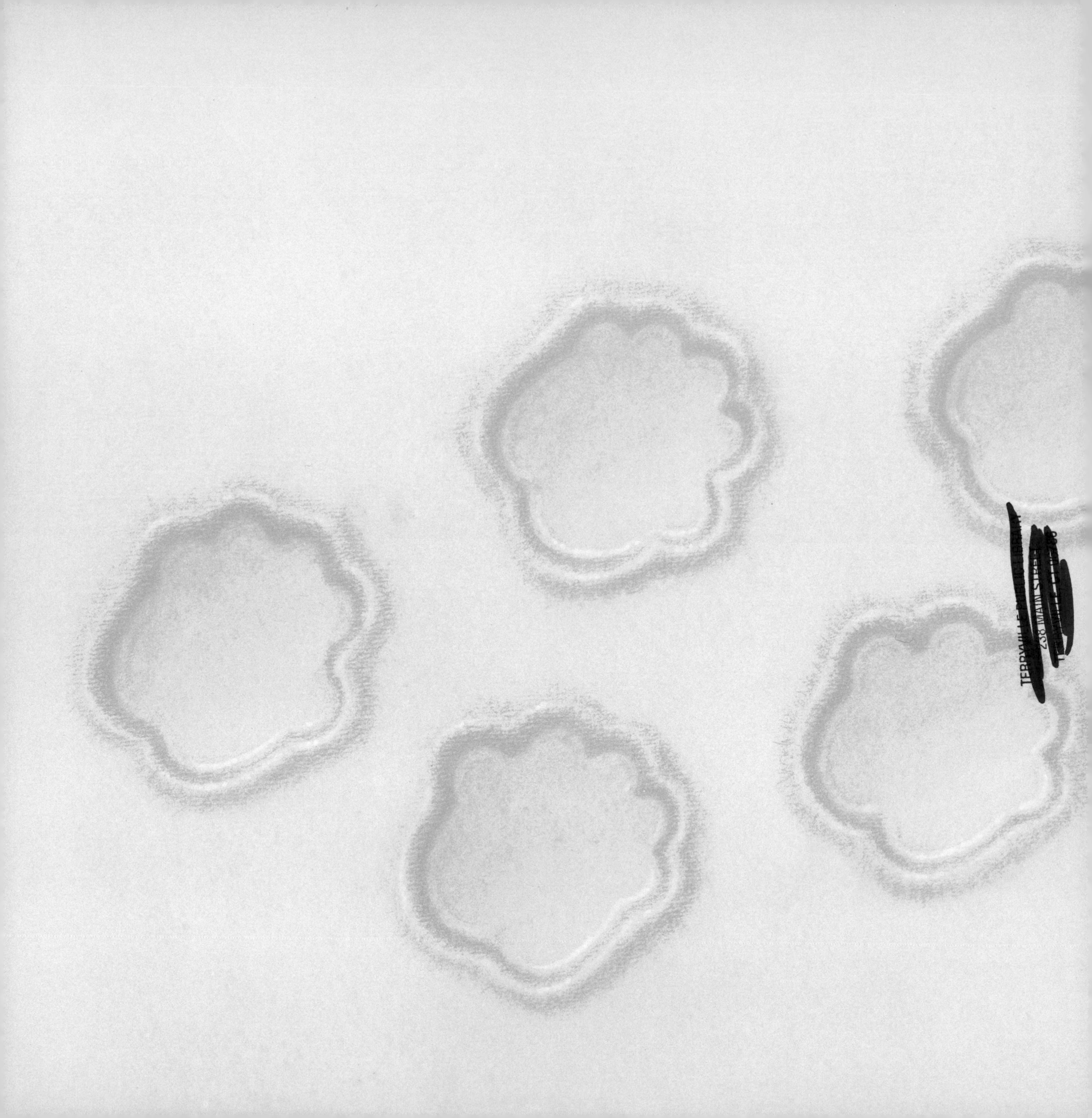